MW00947090

Printed in the United States of America

First Printing, 2018

ISBN: 978-1-7325303-3-1

Dimods Publishing
4935 W Byron Pl Denver, CO 80212

www.blinkybooks.com

Blinky Saves the Sea Turtles is a children's story about the adventure of a determined lightening bug. This funny and engaging story is about a plastic bag that gets caught in the wind and ends up in the ocean half way around the World. The plastic bag sinks into the ocean and looks like a jelly fish where the Grandpa Ridley sea turtle tries to eat it and starts choking. After he is rescued, the sea life learns what the plastic bag is and Blinky learns that his actions can affect the wonderful sea life half way around the World. Kids and grown ups will learn tips and tricks on ways they can help save the sea turtles as well!

Page 5 is dedicated to the loving memory of Great Grandma Broome who painted the side of the page with the barn and the beautiful trees. Thank you for trickling down your inspiration to us. Look Great Grandma, you're a published children's book artist.

In dedication to the loving support of my parents,
love you mostest.
And to all the beating hearts needing our voice.

Dedicated out of respect for our incredible, fragile,
strong and life giving planet (home of the turtles).

Suddenly, a big gust of wind swirled around them and carried Barry's plastic sandwich bag up into the air.

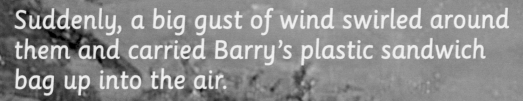

Barry ran after the plastic bag
jumping up trying to catch it.

A little help
over here!

3

Barry & Blinky could not catch the plastic bag.
They sadly watched as it swirled with the wind out of sight.

Don't worry,
I got this!

4

Blinky is super excited that he gets to use his bottom
as a flashlight to keep searching for the plastic bag.

7

8

Blinky was very sad that he was not able to catch the bag.

He watched with sad eyes as the bag filled with water & slowly sank into the ocean.

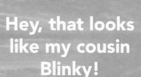

Hey, that looks like my cousin Blinky!

Blinky's cousin el pompis bombilla (*lightbulb bottom*), was out for his morning fly and came across Blinky huffing & puffing.

Hola primo Blinky!

What are you doing here in my part of the world?

Cousin Bombilla! It's been so long!

Blinky tells cousin Bombilla about his great travels trying to catch the plastic bag.

He sadly points to the bag sinking into the ocean.

12

We are here in South America. In this area we speak Spanish.

scutes

The Olive Ridley Sea turtles have a heart shaped shell with 6 or more scutes on each side.

Can you count how many scutes are on this shell?

Look Blinky! There's Grandpa Ridley & Cheloni now. Let's go say hi!

Grandpa Ridley & his granddaughter Cheloni were out swimming for lunch in the deep vast blue ocean.

15

17

18

Suddenly, Grandpa Ridley looks really worried & starts pointing to his mouth. Everyone starts to panic when they see that he is choking.

20

Grandpa Ridley opens his mouth wide
hoping everyone will see what is choking him.

They all gather around & notice a shiny clear
looking something in his throat.

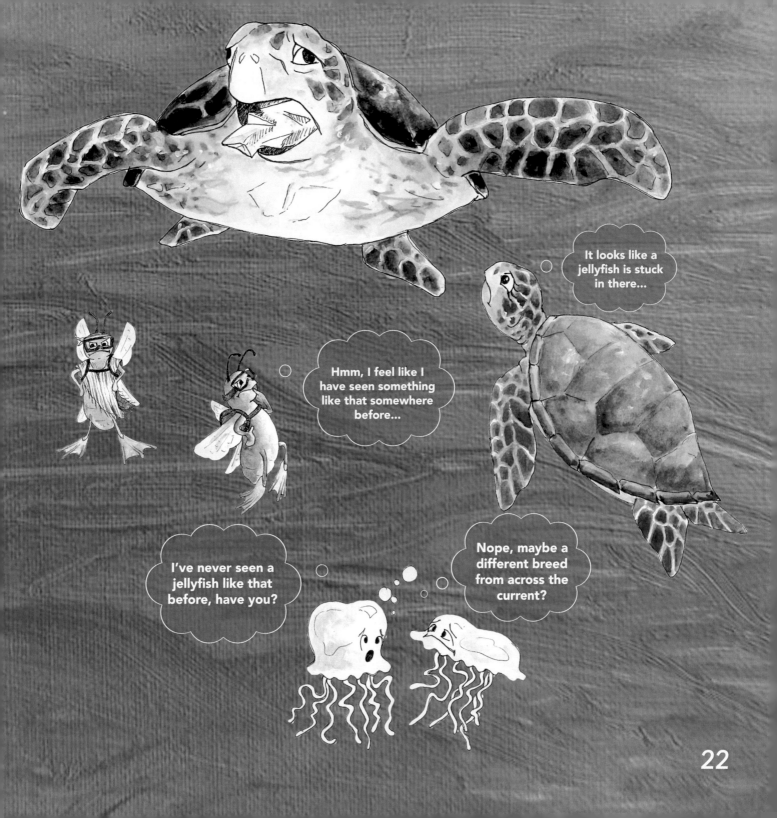

22

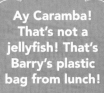

23

Everyone quickly grabbed a part of the plastic bag.

On the count of Español 3, everyone pull!

Please be careful. I would be so sad if anything happened to you!

UNO!
DOS!
TRES!

25

28

My new friend, can you tell us what that was?

Well Señor Ridley, that was a plastic bag. They are used on land to carry and store food...

...I had no idea that our plastic bags could end up way over here in the ocean & harm the sea life.

I'm sorry you almost choked Grandpa Ridley!
I'm so happy you are ok.

I'm grateful to have this new awareness. Now that I know, I will go home & tell my friend Barry what happened. We will research & find new ways to carry and store our food so that it will never hurt you or any other sea life again!

Want to Help the Sea Turtles?

- Use reusable bags for all your shopping needs instead of plastic ones!

- Use fun reusable sandwich bags instead of ziplock baggies.

- Use straws that are compostable or reusable & recyclable

- Hey grown ups, try using mason jars or other glass containers to store food, carry & pack lunches & shop in bulk with!

- Bento boxes are also fun to try & bring to school & work.

- Use sustainable materials that are kind to the planet to produce as well as dispose of.

- Try the new biodegradable wraps & food covers instead of ziplocks or plastic wrap (cellophane).

- Have fun and research your own ways to keep the planet & the wonderful inhabitants happy & safe!

Share what you learn with others at www.blinkybooks.com

The End